London
Symphony
Orchestra

How to Build an
Orchestra

by Mary Auld with the musical support of Rachel Leach

Illustrated by Elisa Paganelli

With an introduction by Sir Simon Rattle

In association with the London Symphony Orchestra

Crocodile Books, USA
An imprint of Interlink Publishing Group, Inc.
www.interlinkbooks.com

Foreword by Sir Simon Rattle

Playing percussion in the Merseyside Youth Orchestra when I was ten was one of the most exciting and inspiring moments of my young life. I discovered early on that there is nothing to compare with a full symphony orchestra for making and sharing the music I love with others.

For this reason, it gives me great pleasure to introduce you to *How to Build an Orchestra*. In it, you can discover the instruments of the orchestra and the amazing music they make. I am delighted by the way the words and pictures interact so well with the provided music from the London Symphony Orchestra (the LSO). The music selection reveals the variety of sounds that each instrument brings as well as the amazing richness of a symphony orchestra's repertoire.

The London Symphony Orchestra's goal is to bring the greatest music to the greatest number of people. This is at the heart of everything that it does and has done for over 100 years. Established in 1904 by a number of London's finest musicians, the LSO is still owned by its Members, 95 brilliant musicians who come from around the world. It is a source of great pride to me that I have been chosen to be Music Director by this extraordinary team.

The work of LSO Discovery, the Orchestra's community and education program, is something to which all of us are particularly committed. It brings the work of the LSO together with all parts of society and engages with many people who would not otherwise have the opportunity to interact with music. Its goals are embodied in our regular schools and family concerts.

How to Build an Orchestra is a further extension of the LSO's aims to make and share music with many. I hope that by reading it and listening to the music, you will discover the true magic that music brings to all our lives.

Enjoy.

Sir Simon Rattle
Music Director, LSO

Contents

Listen

Look out for these panels throughout
the book—and find the music online at
www.lsolive.co.uk/howtobuildanorchestra
using the code HOWTO

Meet the Conductor

This is Simon.
Simon loves music. He loves to listen to it, and loves to make it.

Sometimes Simon hums to himself, sometimes he sings and occasionally he whistles. But that really isn't enough for him—he wants to share music with everyone. That's why he is a conductor. A conductor is the person who leads an orchestra.

An orchestra is made up of lots of musicians playing different musical instruments. The conductor, someone like Simon, makes sure they play together and in time. Simon shows them the speed with a baton. He also shows the orchestra how to feel the music—with his arms, body, and face.

Together, a conductor and an orchestra make beautiful music that everyone can enjoy.

Listen

Track 1: Symphony No. 4 "Italian" is a piece of beautiful music written for the orchestra by Felix Mendelssohn. Here the London Symphony Orchestra plays its first section or movement. See if you can move your hands along with the music.

Simon has been looking at piles of scores. A score is a book with music in it, written with dots on lines. They seem all jumbled up to most of us but Simon reads them as musical notes—the notes to play when you make music.

♯ *A composer has written each of these scores. Composers make up music in their heads and write it down so other people can play it. Over the centuries, men and women have composed lots of different music:*

music that tells stories ...

music that makes you cry ...

music that makes you smile ...

music that makes you dance ...

music that makes you feel things you simply can't put into words.

Listen

Tracks 2 to 6: These are extracts from five pieces. Listen to them and decide which one Simon is listening to in the pictures above. Of course, some of them may do more than one thing! Find their names and composers at the back of the book.

Simon's scores are big. They show him what every instrument in the orchestra is playing and when. When he reads the score, he hears the music in his head.

He has chosen two pieces to perform. He needs an orchestra to play them. But Simon has a problem—he hasn't got an orchestra! He has to build one.

The Auditions

To build an orchestra, Simon has to find lots of talented musicians. He has put out a call to players around the world to come to auditions. He will listen to each one play and then choose his orchestra.

The auditions will take a long time—you need a lot of instruments and a lot of musicians to make a big orchestra. For his two pieces, Simon needs 84 musicians to play all the instruments on his list.

Strings:

14 first violins

12 second violins

10 violas

8 cellos

6 double basses

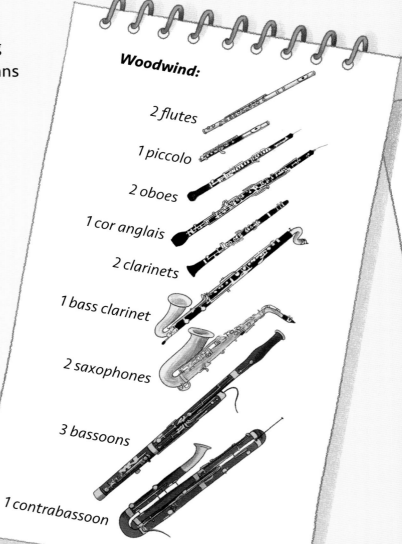

Woodwind:

2 flutes

1 piccolo

2 oboes

1 cor anglais

2 clarinets

1 bass clarinet

2 saxophones

3 bassoons

1 contrabassoon

On the day of the auditions, the hopeful musicians line up. Most bring their instruments with them, including the huge double basses.

ORCHESTRA AUDITIONS
FOR A GREAT PERFORMANCE

TODAY FROM 9

Brass:

4 French horns

4 trumpets

3 trombones

1 tuba

Percussion:

timpani

snare drum

bass drum

crash cymbals

tam-tam

Special section:

harp

celeste

Strings and Bows

The auditions are underway. Simon begins with the string section—the heart of the orchestra. Simon needs violin, viola, cello, and double bass players. These instruments make up the string family—they have four strings and are usually played with sticks called bows.

Cello

Viola

Double bass

Violin

♯ Musicians can play the strings in two different ways ...

by pulling the bow across them ...

or by plucking them—a method called pizzicato.

♯ This makes the strings wobble very, very fast. We say they vibrate—and this makes sound. The hollow wooden box of the instrument makes the sound louder.

The first stringed instrument Simon auditions is the violin. He chooses a leader of the orchestra from the violins.

Simon has found his leader: Roman plays his piece wonderfully and has an excellent bowing technique. He will be the conductor's main support and suggest the best ways to use the bow to the other violinists. He will play a few solos, too!

Listen

Track 7: "The Sea and Sinbad's Ship" is the first movement of **Scheherazade** by Nikolai Rimsky-Korsakov. It has a violin solo played by the leader of the orchestra. Its tune conjures up the princess Scheherazade as she tells a magical story.

After choosing his leader, Simon has to find all the other violinists. Roman will help him. They divide the musicians into two groups—first and second violins.

The violin is the smallest in its family and makes the highest notes. The first violins often play the tunes, or melodies, while the second violins enrich the sound with deeper notes.

♯ *Each string has a different pitch. Pitch describes how high or deep a note is.*

♯ *Pressing down on a string with a finger changes the notes. It makes the string shorter. It wobbles, or vibrates, faster and makes a higher pitch.*

First violins

Second violins

In another room, the viola players are tuning up. Violas are bigger than violins and make a deeper sound. Like the second violins, they often support the melody by playing different notes that blend with it, called harmonies.

Strings need tuning to play the right pitch.

Turning the wooden pegs tightens or loosens the strings, tuning them to a particular note. Tighter = higher; looser = lower.

Occasionally, the viola gets to be the star of the show and plays the tune.

Listen

Tracks 8 to 10: Start with **Partita No. 2 in D Minor** (8) by Johann Sebastian Bach to hear a violin playing completely on its own. Next listen to the viola solo in the first movement of Hector Berlioz's **Harold in Italy** (9). Finally enjoy the harmonies of the violins and violas at the start of **The Nutcracker Suite** by Pyotr Ilyich Tchaikovsky.

Now it's the turn of the cellos to audition—the second largest instrument in the string family. Simon listens to the melody played by the cellist. The piece shows off how the cello can play both very high and very low.

Composers often write concertos for the cello. A concerto is a piece of music where a solo instrument plays the melody backed up by an orchestra.

♯ A cellist sits down to play.

♯ A cello is supported on the floor by a spike.

♯ A string player may wobble their hand as they press on the string to make the note richer— an effect called vibrato.

The double basses are the last of the strings to audition. They are by far the biggest of the string family and their huge body makes a very deep sound. They add great power to the orchestra—and can make the music sound a bit scary!

The double basses provide the bassline in orchestral music— the lowest parts in the harmonies.

♯ The strings on a double bass are thick and heavy.

♯ The bow of a double bass is shorter and fatter than a violin's bow.

♯ Played pizzicato, the double bass is great for playing funky jazz and pop rhythms.

Listen

Tracks 11 to 12: The first movement of Edward Elgar's **Cello Concerto** (11) shows off the instrument's beautiful tone. Listen to the pounding bassline created by the double basses at the start of Béla Bartók's **Divertimento for Strings** (12).

15

Woodwind Colors

The strings are chosen. Simon is ready to add more color to his orchestra's sound—the woodwind section. Musicians blow these instruments to play them. The main woodwind instruments are the flute, clarinet, oboe, and bassoon, but they have big families.

Oboes

Bassoon

♯ *In the past, woodwind instruments were made of wood. Now they can also be made of metal or plastic.*

Flutes

♯ *The sound is shaped as it travels through the instrument.*

Each woodwind instrument has its own special sound. They can play the melody or may add pretty trills and harmonies. In some orchestral pieces, they seem to talk to each other and to the strings, exchanging little phrases of music just like a conversation.

Bassoon

Bass clarinet

The musician blows into or over the instrument's mouthpiece to make sound.

Pressing down on the instruments' keys or covering finger holes changes the note.

Listen

Track 13: "Movement 7, Finale" from Serenade No. 10 by Wolfgang Amadeus Mozart shows off the texture and color of the woodwind. It was written in the 1780s, at a time when the French horn was part of the wind section. There's no flute in the piece, which became more popular in the 19th century.

Clarinets

The flutes are first up in the woodwind auditions. A flautist blows over the hole in the flute's mouthpiece to make a note. The piccolo is its smaller relative. It adds sparkling brilliance to a piece of music.

\# *The short, small piccolo has a higher pitch than the flute.*

\# *The flute is the oldest known instrument. Archaeologists have found a flute made from a mammoth tusk that is over 40,000 years old. It looked quite different from the modern flute.*

Clarinets add a big variety of effects. Sometimes their tone is pure and high, sometimes deep and rich. Saxophones are less common in a classical orchestra but can add smooth melodies, strong rhythm, and edgy harmonies. They are often played in jazz and pop bands.

♯ *There are lots of different sizes of clarinet and saxophone. They all make sound using a single reed.*

Listen

Tracks 14 to 15: The flute's clear tone opens the magic in **Prélude à l'après-midi d'un faune** (14) by Claude Debussy. The clarinet sounds equally romantic but richer in the third movement of Sergei Rachmaninov's Symphony No. 2 (15). Listen carefully for the saxophone 2 minutes 57 seconds into "The Dance of the Knights" (track 3).

♯ *Blowing into the mouthpiece makes the reed vibrate to create a noise.*

♯ *The mouthpiece holds the reed, which is made from a type of cane.*

♯ *The larger, bass clarinet plays low, deep notes, adding rich color to the music.*

The oboe can be easily heard over the rest of the orchestra. Sometimes its sound is joyful, sometimes a little sad. Its larger relative, the cor anglais, plays deeper notes that can be even sadder. Other instruments of the orchestra tune to the oboe.

If you blow the reed without the oboe it sounds like a squeaky duck.

The oboe family has a double reed, made from two pieces of cane, held together by twine.

Most professional oboists and bassoonists make their own reeds, slicing them from a piece of cane. It's tricky to do and not all of them work.

Simon auditions the bassoons and contrabassoons last in the woodwind section. He enjoys their warm, deep tone. These instruments often play the bassline.

♯ *The sound travels a long way, down the bassoon and up again, to make low notes.*

♯ *Bassoonists blow through a double reed attached to a metal tube called a crook.*

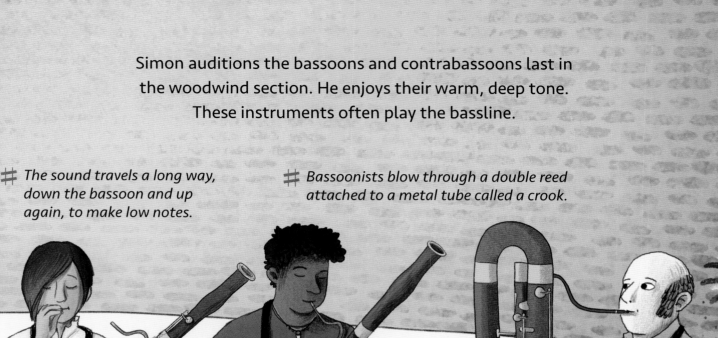

♯ *The contrabassoon plays the deepest notes of the whole orchestra.*

Listen

Tracks 16 and 17: The third movement (16) of **Symphonie fantastique** by Hector Berlioz opens with a conversation between two shepherds—the oboe (off stage) and the cor anglais. Paul Dukas's **The Sorcerer's Apprentice** (17) is a story of magic that goes wrong, when a troop of brooms put under a spell won't stop cleaning. The melody started by the bassoons and contrabassoons creates a sense of the brooms' movement.

The Sound of Brass

Simon is getting excited now. With the strings and woodwind, he can produce sweet melodies and exquisite harmonies. But now he wants to add drama—and a lot of noise. It's time to audition the brass section!

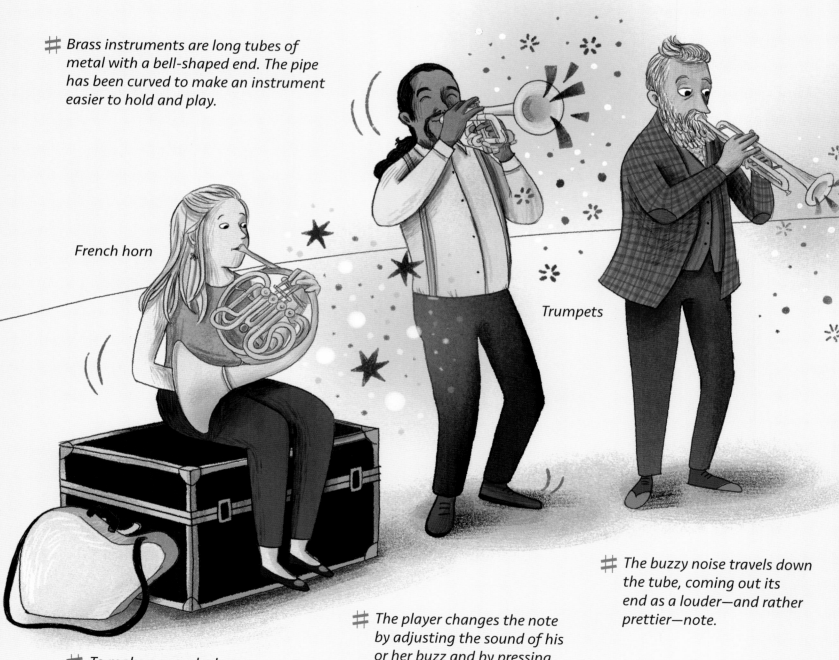

\# *Brass instruments are long tubes of metal with a bell-shaped end. The pipe has been curved to make an instrument easier to hold and play.*

French horn

Trumpets

\# *The buzzy noise travels down the tube, coming out its end as a louder—and rather prettier—note.*

\# *The player changes the note by adjusting the sound of his or her buzz and by pressing down the valves.*

\# *To make a sound a brass player blows a buzzy raspberry with his or her lips into the mouthpiece.*

The brass section is made up of trumpets, French horns, trombones, and tubas. These instruments really are made of brass. Players "buzz" into them to make them sound. Composers can use the brass in their music to sound a warning, stir up a storm, get you dancing, and—just sometimes—to play a sad tune that echoes around the concert hall.

Tuba

Trombone

♯ *Pressing a valve opens up a hole in the tube, which changes the pitch of the note.*

Listen

Track 18: Aaron Copland wrote **Fanfare for the Common Man** for brass instruments and percussion only. A fanfare is a piece of music that gives someone a dramatic entry or introduction. Imagine walking into a crowded room with this playing!

♯ *Trombones use a sliding tube mechanism to change the pitch instead of valves.*

Simon has called the French horns out to the audition first. The French horn started as a hunting horn, and Simon imagines its full tone echoing through the forest. It's not surprising that the French horns often signal the arrival of a hero in film music.

♯ *A player can adjust the pitch with her "buzz," the valves, or by placing her hand in the horn's bell.*

♯ *The rolled-up tube of the French horn measures about 12 feet—as long as a male great white shark.*

Trumpets can play the highest notes of the brass family. Their lively sound is great for sending messages and calling out across the orchestra —just like the first trumpets used to do for an army going into battle.

There are lots of different sizes of trumpet—the smaller the trumpet, the higher the notes it plays.

A trumpeter presses down the valves in different combinations to change the notes.

The tube of a trumpet loops around. A standard-sized tube would be nearly 5 feet long if it was laid straight.

Listen

Tracks 19 and 20: At the start of the Finale (the last part) of **The Firebird Suite** (19) by Igor Stravinsky, the French horn plays a hopeful solo over the strings. The trumpet calls you to attention at the start of Gustav Mahler's Symphony No. 5 (20).

Watch out for the trombones. Played loud, they can add lots of texture to the rhythm of a piece—and lots of excitement. The word trombone comes from the Italian for "large trumpet."

\# *A trombone has a slide: two tubes that slide over each other. The outer tube slides over the inner one to change the pitch.*

\# *Trombones are good for playing a "glissando"— a sound where the pitch slides between two notes.*

\# *The two pipes of a standard tenor trombone measure about 9.75 feet in total.*

\# *There is also a deep bass trombone, which has longer tubing.*

Finally, in the brass section, it's the turn of the tuba—the largest and deepest instrument in its family. A tuba's deep notes can add warm, low harmonies beneath the rest of the orchestra, giving the brass an even rounder sound.

Listen

Track 21: In this extract from the fifth movement of Hector Berlioz's **Symphonie fantastique**, a bell tolls for a funeral; then comes the sound of two tubas playing a sad tune. Trombones and French horns follow. Berlioz used the dark, deep sounds of the brass to achieve a sad but scary effect.

♯ *Laid out straight, the tube of a standard tuba is about 18 feet long—good for making deep notes.*

♯ *A tuba sits on its player's lap. You need a lot of breath to play a tuba!*

♯ *There's usually only one tuba in an orchestra.*

27

Bang! Crash! Percussion!

It's chaos in the audition room. The percussionists have arrived and are setting up their instruments. The percussion is the family of instruments that make their sound by being hit, shaken, or scraped. There are huge drums, bells, cymbals, gongs—and lots more.

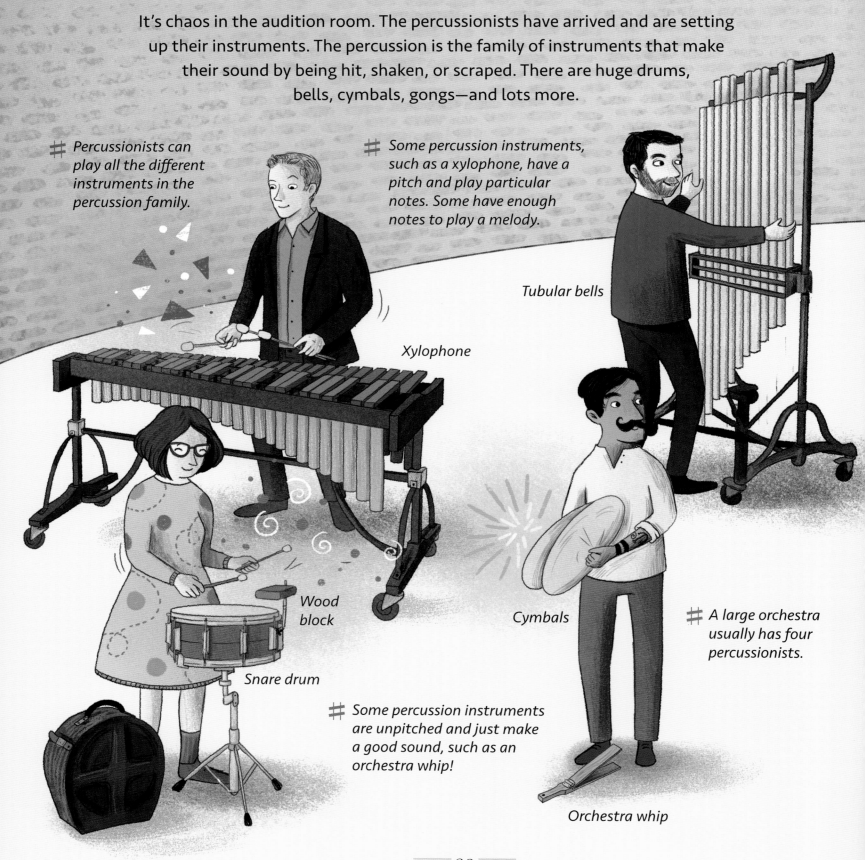

\# *Percussionists can play all the different instruments in the percussion family.*

\# *Some percussion instruments, such as a xylophone, have a pitch and play particular notes. Some have enough notes to play a melody.*

Tubular bells

Xylophone

Wood block

Snare drum

Cymbals

\# *A large orchestra usually has four percussionists.*

\# *Some percussion instruments are unpitched and just make a good sound, such as an orchestra whip!*

Orchestra whip

28

Simon only needs a few percussion instruments for his concert but he wants to hear them all. The percussion section adds a huge variety of noise on top of the rest of the orchestra. Whether heightening the drama or playing the tune, it creates a lot of atmosphere.

♯ The percussion section often gives strong rhythmic force to a piece.

Tambourine

Timpani

Tam-tam

Bass drum

Listen

Track 22: Benjamin Britten wrote **The Young Person's Guide to the Orchestra** to show off all its different instruments. In this section, the percussion plays over the strings using the following instruments: timpani, bass drum, cymbals, tambourine, triangle, snare drum, wood block, xylophone, castanets, tam-tam, and a whip. Can you pick out the crack of the whip?

Drums are great for rhythm—they feature in lots of dance music and keep an army marching. In the orchestra, a drum can open a piece, drive the music on, or bring it to a spectacular climax.

Timpani can be tuned to particular notes.

These drums can play the melody, the harmony, and the rhythm.

To change the note on a drum, the timpanist uses a foot pedal to tighten or loosen its skin.

Listen

Tracks 23 to 25: The timpani gets the Finale (23) of Dmitri Shostakovich's Symphony No. 5 off to a spectacular start. The huge bass drum in the "Dies Irae" (24) of Giuseppe Verdi's **Requiem** sounds a warning—it is the day of anger! The tambourine adds lots of life to "Trepak" (25)—a Russian dance—in Tchaikovsky's **The Nutcracker Suite**. You'll hear the snare drum later (see 32).

A drum has a skin, or membrane, stretched over its body. Percussionists hit the skin with sticks, beaters, or their hands to make the sound. Different drums have different effects but all of them can bring energy to the music.

♯ *Hit a tambourine with your hand, shake it, or use your thumb to make an amazing roll.*

♯ *A snare drum creates two main sounds: one abrupt and rattling made by the metal wires or "snares" stretched across its bottom.*

♯ *Tambourines have metal jingles around their frame. Some, like drums, have skin stretched across them.*

♯ *The percussionist switches off the snares to make the second sound, which is more hollow and open.*

♯ *The bass drum is the biggest percussion instrument. It can be played gently ...*

... but a big bang on the bass drum really attracts your attention.

Sound is all about those wobbly vibrations. Change the vibrations and you change the nature of the sound. Each percussion instrument makes a different noise because of the material it is made from, its shape, and its size, which changes the vibrations.

♯ You can play a single metal cymbal with sticks or beaters to make it vibrate. The harder you hit, the bigger the vibrations and the louder the noise.

♯ A tam-tam is a large, hanging metal disk. You hit it with a padded beater.

♯ Xylophone means "wood sound." A xylophone has pieces of wood arranged in size order to play different notes.

♯ A glockenspiel is like a small xylophone with metal pieces instead of wood. They sound like tinkling bells.

Listen

Tracks 26 to 28: The xylophone leads the way in Aram Khachaturian's **Sabre Dance** (26)—but listen out for cymbals, timpani, and snare drum! Gustave Holst uses the tambourine and then glockenspiel to evoke "Jupiter" in **The Planets** (27). Tubular bells herald the great battle victory at the end of Tchaikovsky's **1812 Overture** (28), followed by a lot of other percussion, including cannons!

♯ *A triangle is a metal bar bent into the shape that gives it its name. It is suspended on a string. You hit it with a metal stick.*

♯ *Hit together the two shell-shaped pieces of castanets to create a clacking noise.*

♯ *Tubular bells are long hollow pipes. Each pipe is a different length and plays a different ringing note when you hit it with a hammer.*

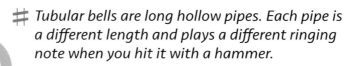

And Finally...

The auditions are nearly over. Simon and Roman have to make some decisions. They may ask some people to play for them again. However there are a few final instruments to hear—ones that don't quite fit in any of the families.

The piano makes a noise by hammers hitting strings inside its body. A pianist presses keys on a keyboard to play a piano. The keys trigger the hammers, which hit the strings.

There are 88 different keys attached to 88 different hammers to play 88 different pitches.

A pianist can play lots of notes at once—so a piano can play the melody, harmonies, and rhythm all at once.

A celeste is a keyboard instrument. The pianist plays it.

The hammers in a celeste hit metal bars that make tinkling, bell-like notes—similar to a glockenspiel.

A harpist plays the harp by pulling the strings. It makes a magical sound.

Each string plays a different note.

A harp has lots of strings— 47—but no bow.

A harpist can change the pitch of a string by pressing one of the seven pedals at the bottom of the harp.

Listen

Tracks 29 to 31: Hear the piano contrast with the orchestra in the first movement (29) of Béla Bartók's **Piano Concerto No. 3**. The tinkly celeste evokes a delicate Sugar Plum Fairy (30) in Tchaikovsky's **The Nutcracker Suite**. Listen how the harp contrasts with the strings at the start of the second movement (31) of Hector Berlioz's **Symphonie fantastique**.

Simon double checks his list—he now has all his instruments and all his musicians. He is a little sad he doesn't need recorders or guitars or a huge drum kit, but that's for another concert. It is time to start rehearsing.

Rehearsals

Simon has put his musicians together, but to build them into a great orchestra they need to practice together—it's a bit like a football team. In rehearsals, the orchestra get to know the music, how each other plays, and they also get to know their boss—the conductor!

♯ *The snare drum starts the piece they are rehearsing. Its strong rhythm never stops, while the melody on top of it is passed around the other instruments— just about everyone gets to be a star.*

Simon has chosen two pieces for his concert. The first is called *Boléro* by Maurice Ravel.
It is a very intense piece, with very rigid timing, that builds and builds to a dramatic climax.
It was written in 1928 for a ballerina. Imagine her dancing to the relentless rhythm.

\# *The piece crescendoes—gets louder and louder—as more instruments play. They must all come in at exactly the right time. Simon signals when.*

\# *But, like Ravel instructed, Simon doesn't want the piece to get faster. He keeps the speed he beats absolutely steady.*

Listen

Track 32: This short extract plays the opening of Maurice Ravel's **Boléro**, establishing the rhythm, bassline, and the melody.

Simon is ready to rehearse the second piece now: the *Pastoral Symphony* by Ludwig van Beethoven. It tells a story without words—one of the first orchestral pieces of music to do this.

The *Pastoral Symphony* has five parts—or movements. It was written in 1808, 110 years before *Boléro*, and has a completely different feel. Some of the instruments used in *Boléro*—such as the saxophone—weren't even invented then.

♯ Beethoven described the first movement as an "Awakening of cheerful feelings on arrival in the countryside." The orchestra is going for a walk ...

♯ Beethoven called the second movement "Scene by a brook." The strings create a sense of a gently flowing river, helped by Simon's gestures.

At its end, the woodwind conjure up birdsong—a flute is the nightingale, an oboe the quail, and two clarinets a cuckoo.

♯ In the third movement, the orchestra meet what Beethoven described as a "merry gathering of country folk."

The brass, helped by cellos and double basses, becomes a country band. Simon beats a clear rhythm for them.

♯ But the party is interrupted by the fourth movement— "Thunder. Storm." Short violin notes sound like rain. The timpani and double basses are perfect for creating a rumble of thunder.

♯ Then lightning flashes through the violins and timpani.

♯ The fifth movement is the calm after the storm. According to Beethoven, it is a "shepherd's song. Cheerful and thankful."

♯ The strings return to the gentle feeling of the first movement.

♯ Toward the end, Simon slows the music to create a sense of a prayer and peace.

Listen

Tracks 33 to 37: These five little extracts come from each of the movements of the **Pastoral Symphony**. (33) The oboes pipe the melody picked up from the strings. (34) Listen to the different birds singing. (35) Now the band is playing. (36) Hear the thunder—and lightning! (37) And finish with the more peaceful sounds of good weather returning.

The Big Night

It's the night of the concert. It will begin with *Boléro*. The hall is packed and the audience watches excitedly as the orchestra come on stage. The oboe plays a note and there is a huge noise as all the other instruments tune to it. Then silence. First Roman and then Simon come on stage to huge applause. Then silence again.

Simon picks up his baton …

And the snare drum begins, with the cellos and violas beneath.

The violas are played pizzicato, sideways on—a bit like guitars.

Now the bassoon comes in with the next part of the melody.

The flute starts the melody, and the clarinet picks it up.

The harp adds harmony to the cellos and violas.

And still the snare drum plays …

Simon brings in the saxophones —there are two sizes—first the tenor and then the soprano.

The melody passes around— the E-flat clarinet, the oboe, the flute again.

Now all the strings are playing the pizzicato bassline. It's getting louder.

The audience is completely hypnotized as the piccolo, French horn, and celeste pick up the melody.

The oboes and clarinets follow, and now the trombones slide in.

Simon keeps that steady pace.

Roman and the first violins take the tune.

Simon brings the trumpets in—they turn up the volume.

The woodwind and violins build the melody once again. The timpani is adding to the bass.

Now everyone is playing. A change in the music pitch adds a clever twist ...

And the music comes to its crashing end. Then silence. The audience wakes from its trance—and the applause begins.

Listen

Track 38: This is the whole of **Boléro**. See if you can follow the pictures and the music together.

The night finishes with the *Pastoral Symphony*. All the practicing pays off. Just like Simon wanted, he and the orchestra share the music they love with the audience. The listeners are carried away on a musical adventure. They hear ...

music that tells a story ...

music that makes them smile ...

42

music that makes them jump ...

music that makes them dance ...

Listen

Tracks 39 to 43: This is the **Pastoral Symphony, Symphony No.6** by Ludwig van Beethoven, in full—it's 42 minutes in total. Try starting with one movement.

music that makes them cry and feel a sense of bliss.

As Simon bows and listens to the applause, he feels proud. He has built an orchestra. Together they have made beautiful, fabulous music that everyone can enjoy. He can't wait for the next concert.

A Symphony Orchestra

This is a pictogram of a full-size symphony orchestra, such as the London Symphony Orchestra, showing the main instruments, their players, and where they usually sit. The instruments and numbers needed can change from piece to piece, just like between *Boléro* and the *Pastoral Symphony*.

Timpani

Percussion

French horns

Clarinets

Harp

Flutes

Piano

Second violins

First violins

Trombones

Bassoons

Tuba

Oboes

Trumpets

Violas

Cellos

Double
basses

Conductor

About the Music

Disc 1: Track 1 Symphony No. 4 in A Major "Italian," Mvt I. Allegro Vivace by Felix Mendelssohn (1809–1847). This piece was first performed in 1833. It was inspired by a visit to Italy, a place Felix found full of color and joy. While writing it, he predicted, "It will be the jolliest piece I have ever done ... ."

Track 2 *The Swan of Tuonela* (Lemminkäinen Suite) by Jean Sibelius (1865–1957). This beautiful 1895 tone poem could well make you cry—it evokes a swan swimming through a scary, magical kingdom.

Track 3 *Romeo and Juilet* Suite No. 2, "Montagues and Capulets" by Sergei Prokofiev (1891–1953). This music tells a story of knights dancing at a ball before a fight so is often called "The Dance of the Knights." It was originally part of a 1938 ballet based on Shakespeare's play, *Romeo and Juliet*.

Track 4 *Daphnis et Chloé*, "Dawn" by Maurice Ravel (1875–1937). This 1912 piece shows how music can conjure up feelings beyond words. Ravel captures in the ballet music the magic of a sunrise at dawn.

Track 5 "Unsquare Dance" by Dave Brubeck (1920–2012). This famous 1961 jazz piece is in the very "unsquare" and unusual time of 7. Try counting along as you dance!

Track 6 "Tritsch Tratsch Polka," by Johann Strauss II (1825–1899). This fast piece of music will make you smile. Its title refers to how people like to gossip. Strauss wrote over 500 waltzes and polkas.

Track 7 *Scheherazade*, Symphonic Suite, Mvt I. "The Sea and Sinbad's Ship," by Nikolai Rimsky-Korsakov (1844–1908). This suite was inspired by the stories of *One Thousand and One Nights* which includes the adventures of Sinbad the Sailor.

Track 8 Partita No. 2 in D Minor for solo violin, Mvt I. Allemande by Johann Sebastian Bach (1685–1750). This is the first movement in a piece that many consider one of the most beautiful ever written for solo violin.

Track 9 *Harold in Italy*, Mvt I. "Harold in the Mountains" by Hector Berlioz (1803–1869). This piece was written to show off the sound of a new viola owned by the famous soloist Niccolò Paganini (1782–1840).

Track 10 *The Nutcracker Suite*, Miniature Overture by Pyotr Ilyich Tchaikovsky (1840-1893). This is the orchestral opening to the famous 1892 ballet. It is light and frothy, just like the ballet.

Track 11 Cello Concerto in E Minor, Mvt I. Adagio - Moderato by Edward Elgar (1857–1934). Written in 1919, just after the end of the First World War, this piece was first performed by the LSO. For many, it captures the sadness of this time.

Track 12 Divertimento for Strings, Sz. 113, Mvt I. Allegro ma non troppo by Béla Bartók (1881–1945). Hungarian composer Bartók was influenced by the baroque music of the 17th century when he wrote this piece in 1939. He wrote he felt like "a musician from the past."

Track 13 Serenade No. 10 or "Gran Partita," Mvt VII. Finale. Molto allegro by Wolfgang Amadeus Mozart (1756–1791). This piece was described as "glorious and grand" by someone who heard it in 1784, soon after it was written.

Track 14 *Prélude à l'après-midi d'un faune (Prelude to the Afternoon of a Faun)* by Claude Debussy (1862–1918). This 1894 piece for flute and orchestra was inspired by a poem about a faun (a mythical half-man, half-goat creature) dreaming on a sunny afternoon. Many saw it as revolutionary, inspiring a new way of writing music.

Track 15 Symphony No. 2 in E Minor, Mvt III. Adagio by Sergei Rachmaninov (1873–1943). Rachmaninov's first symphony had been a disaster and he wrote this one was a "severe worry" to him until it was performed to great acclaim in 1908.

Track 16 *Symphonie fantastique*, Mvt III. "Scene in the Fields" by Hector Berlioz (1803–1869). This 1830 symphony tells a story of a poor artist with a broken heart. Berlioz said the shepherd's duet at the start of this third movement gives the artist hope. See also **Tracks 21** and **31**.

Track 17 *The Sorcerer's Apprentice* by Paul Dukas (1865–1935). This French piece, written in 1897, captures the chaos caused by a foolish trainee wizard. You can hear marching broomsticks, sloshing water, and magic within the music.

Track 18 *Fanfare for the Common Man* by Aaron Copland (1900–1990). This stirring piece was written in 1942 to boost people's spirits during the Second World War.

Track 19 *The Firebird Suite*, Mvt XV. Finale by Igor Stravinsky (1882–1971). This music was written as a 1910 ballet based on Russian fairy tales, where a magic firebird helps a prince defeat Kachtcheï, an evil wizard. In the final scene, everyone celebrates because the wizard is gone.

Track 20 Symphony No. 5, Mvt I. by Gustav Mahler (1860–1911). This great and intense symphony was written between 1901 and 1902, reflecting Mahler's feelings as he fell in love with his future wife, Alma.

Track 21 *Symphonie fantastique*, Mvt V. "Witches' Sabbath" by Hector Berlioz (1803–1869). See **Track 16**. In this nightmare movement, the artist dreams he is at his own funeral. Berlioz wrote it was attended by a "hideous gathering of ghosts, sorcerers, and monsters."

Track 22 *The Young Person's Guide to the Orchestra*, Variation M. Percussion by Benjamin Britten (1913–1976). This piece was written for a 1946 film called *The Instruments of the Orchestra* that starred the LSO. Britten introduced all the different parts of the orchestra through a series of variations (versions) on a theme by another British composer, Henry Purcell (1659-1695).

Track 23 Symphony No. 5 in D Minor, Mvt IV. Allegro non troppo by Dmitri Shostakovich (1906–1975). Shostakovich wrote this in 1937 when the strict Russian government said that all music must be celebratory and triumphant, so Shostakovich added a very, very happy ending, introduced by the timpani. We now know he was being sarcastic and it was not how he really felt.

Track 24 Requiem, No. 2 *Dies Irae* by Giuseppe Verdi (1813–1901). Verdi was well-known for his opera, so his 1874 Requiem (a piece of music sung at a Catholic funeral) is full of drama and passion. It is usually performed with a huge choir and a full symphony orchestra.

Track 25 *The Nutcracker Suite*, IV. "Trepak" by Pyotr Ilyich Tchaikovsky (1840–1893). This part of the famous ballet accompanies a lively Russian folk dance.

Track 26 *Gayenah*, "Sabre Dance" by Aram Khachaturian (1903–1978). This fast and furious music comes from a 1942 Russian ballet, where the performers leap and dance with swords called sabres.

Track 27 *The Planets*, Mvt IV. "Jupiter, the Bringer of Jollity" by Gustav Holst (1874–1934). The LSO gave the first complete performance of Holst's seven-movement suite in 1920. This movement is a celebration of the planet Jupiter, named after the king of the gods in Roman mythology.

Track 28 *1812 Overture*, by Pyotr Ilyich Tchaikovsky (1840–1893). Led by Napoloeon, the French army invaded Russia in 1812 but was defeated. This piece, written in 1880, celebrates the Russian army's great victory.

Track 29 Piano Concerto No. 3 in E Major, Mvt I. Allegretto by Béla Bartók (1881–1945). Bartók wrote this piece shortly before he died as a birthday present for his wife. Even though he was ill, it is full of life. This first movement has a folk music theme from Hungary, Bartók's home country.

Track 30 *The Nutcracker Suite*, IV. "Dance of the Sugar Plum Fairy" by Pyotr Ilyich Tchaikovsky (1840–1893). This piece from the famous ballet is well-known for the way a ballerina dances to it on pointe—the very tips of her toes.

Track 31 *Symphonie fantastique*, Mvt II. "A Ball" by Hector Berlioz (1803–1869). See **Track 16**. In this movement, the artist attends a ball. The magical harp introduction leads to a waltz, a popular dance of the era.

Disc 2: Tracks 32, 38 *Boléro* by Maurice Ravel (1875–1937). Short extract (32); full piece (38). Ravel wrote this piece for the Russian ballerina Ida Rubinstein (1885-1960) who danced at its first performance in Paris

in 1928. When Ravel first had the idea of the melody, he thought it had an "insistent quality" that needed to be repeated, almost like a spell—so he does, round and around for over 10 minutes. The only thing that changes are the instruments that play it and the volume. Ravel therefore created the longest crescendo in the history of music.

Tracks 33-37, 39-43 Symphony No. 6 in F Major, *Pastoral Symphony* by Ludwig van Beethoven (1770–1827). Short extracts (33-37); full symphony (39-43). This symphony was inspired by Beethoven's love of walks in the countryside outside Vienna, Austria, where he lived. He called it, in full, "Pastoral Symphony, or Recollections of Country Life." It was first performed in 1808 in the same concert as his *Symphony No.5*, which is famous for its passion and strong emotions. The *Pastoral Symphony* still has plenty of drama but it is really about the joy Beethoven found in nature. And although there is a story, as Beethoven wrote, for him the piece is all about "feelings" rather than "pictures."

Glossary

audition – like an interview, a formal meeting where a musician plays to show off his or her skill

baroque – relating to the style of music and art of the 17th and 18th centuries in Europe

bassline – the bottom part of a piece

baton – a thin stick used by a conductor to direct an orchestra

bow – the wooden stick with horsehair stretched across its length used to play stringed instruments such as the violin

brass – the name of the family of wind instruments made of brass

composer – someone who writes, or composes, music

concerto – a piece for orchestra and usually one soloist (often in three movements)

conductor – the person who directs an orchestra or choir

crescendo – gradually getting louder

glissando – a continuous sound created by sliding between two notes

harmony – the way two notes or tunes mix when played together

key – on a musical instrument, a part you press to change the note

keyboard – a set of keys grouped together on a musical instrument such as a piano

melody – a line of musical notes that makes a satisfying shape, or a musical sentence, sometimes called the tune

mouthpiece – the part of a musical instrument placed on or near the mouth

movement – one section of a larger piece

peg – the pegs on a stringed instrument which are turned to tighten or loosen its strings

percussion – something struck or shaken to make a sound; the family of instruments played in this way

pitch – sound described as high and low

pizzicato – plucking the strings of an instrument

reed – one or two pieces of cane used to make the sound on most woodwind instruments

rhythm – a collection of notes of different duration forming a pattern

score – music written down showing all the different parts and instruments playing; a visual representation of the music

solo – a prominent part played by one musician alone

strings – the family of musical instruments that use strings to make their sound

symphony – a large piece for orchestra (often in four movements)

tone – the quality of a sound

tone poem – a piece of music for orchestra that describes a story, picture, or mood and is usually one movement

trill – a fast wobble between two pitches

valve – a part of a brass instrument which the musician presses to change the note

vibration – a very fast wobble

vibrato – a slight wavering change of pitch to color the sound

wind instrument – a musical instrument that a player blows to make sound

woodwind – the family of wind instruments originally made of wood

Index

First American edition published in 2020 by
CROCODILE BOOKS
an imprint of Interlink Publishing Group, Inc.
46 Crosby St., Northampton, MA 01060
www.interlinkbooks.com

Copyright © Hodder and Stoughton, 2020
Illustrations copyright © Hodder and Stoughton, 2020
Text copyright © Hodder and Stoughton, 2020
Introduction © Sir Simon Rattle, 2020
Recordings © LSO LIVE LTD
Music © 2001 – 2017 London Symphony Orchestra Ltd only

Originally published in Great Britain in 2020 by Wayland,
an imprint of Hachette Children's Group

All rights reserved.

Design by Peter Scoulding
Edited by Rachel Cooke and Paul Rockett
Music consultancy by Rachel Leach on behalf of the London Symphony Orchestra

Any likenesses to members of
the London Symphony Orchestra
are created with their full permission.

MIX
Paper from
responsible sources
FSC® C104740
FSC
www.fsc.org

Library of Congress Cataloging-in-Publication data available
ISBN 978-1-62371-871-8

Printed and bound in China